REDEMPTION

NICKITA CAMPBELL

ISBN: 978-1-7357977-0-0

For permission contact:

blessedbeauty356@gmail.com

Publisher: The Student Teacher, LLC

P.O. Box 813 SAVAGE, MD 20763

www.simenewalden.com

To my loving grandparents Bassell & Adelle Gordon.

I love and miss you.

Nickita Campbell

Redemption: (pronounced ree demp shun)

The action of saving or being saved from sin, error, or evil.

"This is God's plans for the redemption of His world".

Greek word connecting to redemption is "Lutroo" meaning to obtain release by the payment of a price.

Table Of Contents

MYA WILLOUGHBY

For better or for worse huh? When will this sham of a marriage get any better? I was up all night pacing, wondering, and calling Robert's phone frantically but there was still no answer. By the forty-seventh try, the phone was now switched off. I was furious with Robert to say the least; he had promised me that the last time would be the last time. It was now 7:00 am Sunday morning and the kids would soon be up for church. Well, let me go get ready for church because Lord knows only GOD can save this marriage.

At 9:00 am, the children and I were dressed to the nines in our Sunday's best; eating breakfast in our beautiful spacious Victorian-style kitchen. I heard the keys in the door; my heart froze, wondering if I should yell, scream, fight, or should I just end this misery of a marriage with the divorce papers neatly tucked away in my top drawer. Tears filled my eyes as I looked down at the only blessings in our marriage: our children, Carter and Robert Jr. Robert walked into the kitchen and threw his keys down on the marble island. "Daddy, Daddy," the boys squealed.

I took a sip of my coffee and dryly said, "Good Morning Pastor Willoughby, it's time for church."

Robert and I were married for twenty-four years. At the age of forty-four what was I going to do now with my life? I reluctantly retired as a successful business owner once Robert became increasingly successful. I, Mya Michelle Willoughby had the number one top Real Estate businesses in Georgia. I was an extremely successful, powerful, and beautiful woman. I was thick in all the right places with long jet-black flowing hair, pretty full lips, and hazel green eyes. I was told that my beautiful golden complexion looked like I had been kissed by God himself. My husband was a very prominent and influential pastor in Georgia. He was very well established and highly respected. I gave up my successful businesses only to become his First Lady. Robert was a great man but his appetite for women destroyed our marriage years ago. Never in a million years would I have thought I would become the cliché of staying with a man simply because I bore his children. It was all true that I did, in fact, love and adored the life we once had. Our marriage was once filled with love and endless hours of love making; nowadays, our life was filled with quickies and a third or fourth person in our marriage. Our sex life use to be great, it was absolutely mind-blowing but Robert's appetite could not be quenched by just one woman, no matter how hard he tried. Our congregation started to suspect something was up when his receptionist just up and left the church and her position. Ms. Jasmine Hill was a beautiful 26-year-old with long beautiful, golden hair and even longer legs that I found wrapped around my husband's neck one Friday night. Robert swore that it was the first time and against my better judgment, I foolishly believed him.

Now, as I sit here as his new personal assistant, how do I tell Robert this secret that I have been carrying? Will he ever forgive me? Can I even forgive myself? God, please help me as I don't know what to do. This secret I've been concealing will ruin our lives, especially Robert's. What was I thinking? Why did I have to get revenge? Why didn't I just walk away with my children and half of our 200 million dollars in the bank? I'm in too deep now, so it's either sink or swim. I'm not ready to do this but with my loaded silver pistol inside of the manila envelope, I put my sunglasses on and drove directly to meet "him" at our usual coffee spot. I had the documents and the sum of $250,000 in hush money. I can't let Robert as well as our nosey congregation find out, especially our Assistant Pastor Joshua Livingston. Joshua never thought that I was good enough to be the First Lady. If anyone found out what I was so desperately trying to hide, it would ruin me; it could ruin all of us. I could not take that chance. I worked too hard to create this new life and I planned to remove anyone in my path who tried to stop me. I patted the pistol as I stepped inside the coffee shop. Oh Lord, what was I about to do? Could I really go through with this? Just the thought of losing my children reassured me that I can and will do everything in my power to make this problem go away. God would forgive me again, right?

ROBERT WILLOUGHBY

"**Y**ou know that I love my wife and family, so stop calling my phone, stop coming to this church. We are over. I gave you the money you asked for, now get out."

Jasmine laughed. She was obsessed with me but who could blame her: I was 6'2 tall, dark, and handsome. I did things to her that caused her to speak in different languages but I really do love my wife and I'm trying really hard to make it work. This lust problem has gotten the better of me. I thought I had it under control but the moment Jasmine walked into my office, I just knew I had to have her too. Mya doesn't even know about the countless women who left our congregation that didn't just up and "relocate."

Right then, Jasmine's questions snapped me out of my deep thoughts. "Does Mya know about the vacations? Abortions, gifts? You met my family Robert. You can't really believe that I'm walking away just like that. What about this?" She pointed to the 8.5 carat pear-shaped engagement ring that I had given to her foolishly.

"It's yours to keep but I can't marry you. We're over Jasmine."

"OK," she said calmly. "Everyone in this church and I do mean everyone, will know exactly who you really are."

"Are you threatening me?" I asked. "My

congregation loves me and they'll never believe you. I'm the great Robert Bradley Willoughby, Senior Pastor. They would die for me."

Jasmine stormed out of my office and I hit my fist violently on the desk. She could have at least let me in one last time, I thought to myself.

JASMINE HILL

Standing outside of Robert's door, the tears were streaming down my face. I opened my cellphone and watched the last five minutes of our video. Robert had no idea that the last time I videotaped us; this tape showed all the things Pastor Willoughby was doing to me on his desk. It will certainly have everyone believing me. *Ok Pastor Willoughby. You always wanted to be the most famous pastor in Georgia; wait until Channel 61 News gets a hold of this tape. I'm sure*

your face will be everywhere, I thought. I closed my phone and drove directly to the news station. Once I got there, I spoke directly to the leading news correspondent and handed her the incriminating evidence. "Now let's see if even Jesus can save you," I said to myself and laughed.

I felt a twinge of guilt. It wasn't supposed to end this way and I fell head over heels in love with Robert. Oh well. It was time to board my flight and settle in my first-class seat. I was on to destroy the next pastor.

MYA WILLOUGHBY

As I waited in the coffee shop, I thought back on good times with Robert. We met in college and all the girls wanted him. Robert was a communications student, and he also worked at the radio station while earning his degree. With his deep voice on the radio, mixed with his great looks, he had all the girls wanting to intern at the radio station. Plus, it was not easy to be nineteen and fully in love with God. Robert's love for God amazed me. When he saw me reading my bible in the lunchroom, he quoted my favorite proverb.

Proverb 4:7 (KJV*) **"Wisdom is the principal thing; therefore, get wisdom: and with all thy getting, get understanding."**

That very day, we began our romance. Robert led me to the Lord shortly after that. It was incredible being with him: he was sweet, gentle, kind, and loving. However, Robert had another side to him that I discovered. I went to do his laundry as a surprise one day. When I looked in his closet for his laundry bag, thousands upon thousands of pornographic tapes fell onto the floor. He said he was ashamed and was trying to stop. I then thought that by sleeping with him, his addiction would stop. Robert and I both knew that we were going to get married as soon as we graduated, so since he was going to be my husband we were not technically committing sin right?

From the moment I slept with Robert, I was totally hooked. I couldn't get enough of him; his scent, his touch, and his stamina was incredible. Shortly after, Robert said that we couldn't continue what we were doing. I didn't understand that I had only given my body to him. Robert then quoted this scripture to me and I fully understood his view.

1 Corinthians 7:9 (KJV) *"But if they cannot contain, let them marry: for it is better to marry than to burn."*

Robert was right and most importantly; the Word of God is nothing to play with. I loved Robert and he loved me but we had to do the hardest thing, which was stop sleeping together. I begged the Lord to help me because my mind was willing but my flesh was weak.

ROBERT WILLOUGHBY

I knew I could not keep sleeping with Mya but her body called me: it overtook me, consumed me even. It awakened something within me that I couldn't shake off. No one but me will ever experience that drug she possessed. I was hooked and I would die for it.

I had sinned against God by fornicating after promising Him a year prior that I would be celibate until marriage. Unfortunately, I slipped up with Mya and felt horrible about it. I prayed, fasted, and read my Bible but all I could do was think about sleeping with her, having her. I couldn't contain myself and even lost my job at the radio station behind it. I could no longer focus as the cravings and desires got the best of me. The Associate Director noticed a change in my behavior when she approached me to talk. I quickly dismissed the lustful thoughts in my mind but the way her behind looked in that pencil skirt, it was calling me. I fought the urge to pick her up and slam her right on my desk. The decision was made that I would resign that day.

I couldn't stop thinking about being with Mya, so by the next month, we were married. Our wedding was beautiful as my mother spared no expense. I had received my trust fund in the amount of $250,000.00, so money was no longer an issue. Although my father walked out on my mother and I, he left us with a large sum of money from his huge settlement it was the least he could do. I was to receive it on my wedding day.

The first three years of marriage was bliss but I felt that "other appetite" growing again. When that hunger arose, Mya alone could not fulfill me. She tried her very best but to no avail and I sought outside "help."

I had laid on that hotel's massive king size bed thinking about what just happened and how good it felt. I really needed that release as the water in the shower stopped. I was ready for round three, four, and five. Just as I was about to begin again, my phone rang. "Honey my water broke," Mya said.

I was angry as I was still hungry but I had to be there for the birth of our first child. However, I just could not deny "him." It seems like the more I fed this other appetite the hungrier he became he was never satisfied. I threw my companion on the bed and ripped her towel off violently.

"What about your wife and the baby," she asked.

"Let me worry about that. I'm hungry again," I said slyly.

Almost two hours later, with my wife at the hospital getting ready to give birth, I called Mya. "Honey, hang on, I'm twenty minutes away; I had a flat tire." I felt horrible lying to her yet again but this other appetite was growing stronger and stronger by the minute. I shook the thought out of my mind and proceeded to do 90 mph on the highway, racing to the hospital. I made it in time. Mya was dilating and the doctor said that it would be hours before my son would arrive. I told Mya that I was going to find parking and would be back as fast as possible.

I was happy to become a dad and so many thoughts invaded my mind at once. Would my son be just like me? Would he have this appetite also? I tried hard not to become my adulterous, conniving father but to no avail; I turned out just like him. Since I knew the Word of God, I knew all too well about generational curses. My father's love for other women destroyed not just our relationship but his marriage to my mother. *No, my son would be different,* I thought.

My other appetite was still hungry with Mya being so heavily pregnant; she didn't want me coming near her the last couple of weeks.

"Excuse me nurse," I said to the gorgeous nurse who sashayed by, swishing those thick hips from left to right. She turned around and from the looks in her eyes and her very seductive smile, I knew one thing was apparent: I would not be hungry for long.

AHLISA COLBERT

I loved being the Willoughby's nanny for the past five years. Although I was only part-time, they showed me so much love. I accompanied the family on their vacations. We traveled to Dubai, London, Hawaii, and Turks & Caicos. I wondered when I would ever be able to afford these lavish trips. Every time we went away, Pastor Willoughby spent frivolously on jewelry, spas, and private jets. I knew that the church was established but I wondered if they knew that he and his wife spent money like this. They spent thousands of dollars on twenty-four karat gold facials and ten thousand dollars for designer shoes and bags.

As I broke into Pastor Willoughby's private bedroom safe, I took pictures of everything: receipts, paperwork, and every document under the church's name. I videotaped as well. They had to pay because you can't steal from God's people and get away with it. I felt terrible for going along with this as we all had become great friends. It was more like family honestly but I had a job to do and this needed to end. This would be the only way that the church would be saved.

I was about to close the safe when I saw a file with the name Jasmine Hill.

I just had to look into the folder. I saw a sonogram and a birth certificate with Mr. Willoughby's name listed as the father of

Jasmine's child. It didn't stop there; there were pictures of Jasmine in lingerie, letters, and more pictures of them doing things in the house of God that would make anyone repent. I took pictures of it all. Suddenly I saw a cellphone and my curiosity got the best of me. I knew that I shouldn't be doing this but with the children napping in their room, my curiosity got the best of me and the Willoughby's would not be back until later on tonight.

I turned the phone on successfully and no passcode was required. My mouth hung open when I discovered that preaching wasn't the only thing Pastor Willoughby did well. He completely devoured Jasmine like a hungry animal. The way he contorted and manipulated her body for his animalistic pleasure was out of this world and Jasmine was enjoying every single moment. Mr. Willoughby had no mercy on Jasmine as she didn't seem to mind. I pulled the phone forward to get a better view. I saw something in the background and zoomed in, watching it four times. *No it could not be, I knew I was seeing wrong, I didn't just see that*, I thought. Tears streamed down my face. I was blindsided. The air left the room and my body stiffened in sheer disbelief. I was frozen. I did not hear the car drive into the garage or the keys being thrown down on the marble table in the foyer. The only thing I heard was him.

"What are you doing in here," Pastor Willoughby shouted. He stormed into his bedroom with no shoes on. He grabbed the phone out of my hands and locked his bedroom door. Looking straight into my eyes with sheer evil, he uttered two words: "HOW MUCH?"

"What?" I replied in disbelief.

"How much?" he reiterated. "What's it going to cost to keep you quiet?"

Shaking like a leaf, I felt lost, hurt, and afraid. The rage in his eyes assured me he would harm or even kill me if anyone saw him doing the unthinkable. I was lost in thought and the next thing I felt was a black 9mm pistol pressed against my forehead. "How much?" he demanded again. His eyes glared at me angrily as he cocked the gun back. "I won't ask you again."

JOSHUA LIVINGSTON

I took great pride in being the Assistant Pastor to the largest mega church in Atlanta. I love the Lord and I loved serving His people. I grew up in the gritty streets of Brooklyn, Bedford-Stuyvesant to be exact. My mother was on drugs and never knowing my dad, the streets raised me. It was rough from the time I came out of the womb. I was heavily addicted to crack and shuffled in and out of the system my entire life. My mother eventually died of an overdose so I became cold as no one wanted me.

The one thing I did right was get straight A's in school. I received a scholarship to go to college and that's where I met Pastor Robert Willoughby as a freshman while he was a senior. His love for God inspired me and he showed me genuine brotherly love. He showed me how much God truly loves me. I wondered how he knew that I'd never heard the words "I love you" from anyone. I sought God with all my heart and wanted nothing more than to please Him.

However, it seems the tables had turned the more I tried to live Holy and do what's right in the eyes of the Lord, the more Robert strayed away from God. His other appetite, as he would call it, was getting the best of him. As I sit here cleaning up Robert's mess yet again, I couldn't help but think to myself what I was doing here. If anyone found out I was here, it would be a huge scandal. I loved Pastor Rob but him not being able to control his appetite was causing some concern with some of our members.

I had my own problems to worry about; my desire to become the senior pastor filled my mind. There was so much that I wanted to do and improve but Robert was more concerned with women and money, instead of being a great shepherd. Mya was emotionally damaged and she was a horrible first lady. Between her high stiletto heels, designer bags and terrible attitude, the women in the church couldn't relate to her. I know that she's been in a hell of a marriage for over twenty years but she displayed neither love nor affection for her daughters in Christ.

I needed to change how we did things but convincing the great Robert B. Willoughby to step down would be a fight. Robert loved the praise, money, and rising fame he received. I was growing tired of doing his dirty work; whether it was booking hotel rooms for his so-called private conferences or sending flowers to other women. I also had to pay off the last four young ladies who wanted to keep their babies to relocate and that was the final straw. I was going to speak to him about this immediately because this charade had to end. "I will do it this weekend", I said.

As I sat next to one of his victims sobbing softly, I consoled her just like I did all the others. Her name was called Ms. Blake. I saw her off to the room and was told I could not come in. Unfortunately I knew this procedure all too well. This was the last time I would accompany one of his mistresses here again. I was done with these abortion clinics and even more done with Pastor Robert B. Willoughby.

I made a very important phone call before I drove off to meet the perfect person to help me with my plan. "Hey it's me. Call me back **ASAP**."

Yes, Ms. Jasmine Hills definitely would be

interested to hear what I had to say. I called my friend Ahlisa and left a message. "Lisa it's me, call me. Do you have the information that we need yet? Call me back."

AHLISA COLBERT

I almost didn't make it out of the house alive. Pastor Willoughby was so angry and I could still feel the gun imprint on my temple. I still tasted the barrel of the gun in my mouth. I knew for sure that he would kill me right there had it not been for his next-door neighbor that rang the doorbell.

While he was talking to his neighbor, I calmly said, "Goodnight Mr. Willoughby," with all the incriminating evidence in my hands. I smiled slyly and all the time his neighbor never knew what just transpired.

Pastor Willoughby clenched his teeth and said, "Oh, wait one minute please."

I just pushed past him and jumped in my car quickly. I knew I was fired but bringing down a lying, cheating pastor would be my reward.

I drove quickly, heading straight to Joshua's house. I was so excited to deliver all of this evidence to our new soon-to-be Senior Pastor Mr. Joshua Livingston. As I sat in traffic, tears flooded my eyes thinking about the tape. What I saw was unbelievable, it was sickening. Maybe my eyes were playing tricks on me but in my heart of hearts, I knew that it was not. "How could he do such a thing?" The tears flowed even harder. The congregation and his wife would be devastated.

I was so deep in thought that I did not hear the

tractor trailer honking at me; I only felt the impact of being hit. My burgundy Jeep Wrangler flipped four times before landing in a ditch. I began to smell the intense scent of gas. I was in excruciating pain, pinned inside and couldn't get out. The seatbelt was now wrapped tightly around my neck. Suddenly out of nowhere a stranger broke my driver side window and unraveled the seatbelt from my neck, I was able to breathe a little easier. A loud boom invaded my ears; a burning hot sensation ripped my chest apart. I held on tightly to the manila envelope containing the information. The pain was too much. I couldn't catch my breath as blood filled my lungs. "No Lord, please don't let it end like this," I cried. Don't let him get away with this. I struggled harder and harder to breathe. Darkness filled everywhere suddenly; a peace that surpassed all human understanding overtook me as I slurred my last words: **"Lord, receive me into your Kingdom."**

ROBERT WILLOUGHBY

I couldn't believe that little ungrateful, conniving witch, Ahlisa, broke into my private bedroom safe a week ago. *How did she know the combination? How did she know that I had a private safe?* I pondered. Not even my wife knew about that safe. Well, no need to worry about that now. To make matters worse, she got away with all the evidence. I decided right then and there to destroy any evidence that would incriminate me. I went downstairs to my private computer and deleted all of the private statements, messages, emails and videos .The only thing I could not delete was my profile on a very private, elite dating site, where I met Ms. Kendall Scott. She is a beautiful 22-year-old beauty. Kendall was gorgeous, tall, thick, with luscious black hair and brown eyes which left me in a trance. I know I shouldn't feel this way about another woman but Mya and I no longer had any connection let alone intimacy. Don't get me wrong, I still found my wife highly attractive. Mya has a body that would put a twenty-year-old to shame and a face that would win first prize in any beauty competition.

Mya would no longer allow me to touch her. Anytime I attempted to touch her Mya would just push me off. We had no spark left and it was all due to my infidelity. We barely spoke two words to one another. I was now sleeping in the guest bedroom, so she left me no choice but to go somewhere else. I do have needs right? Now

Kendall, on the other hand, promised me maximum pleasure when she arrived from Chicago this Friday. We've been talking, texting, and sending pictures to one another for three months now; she assured me that she was worth the wait. Kendall would never send me the kinds of pictures I wanted but the tasteful pictures that she did send was enough to intrigue and entice me. My body yearned for her badly.

Everything was set. I paid for the finest hotel, first class ticket, and the most exclusive restaurant here in Georgia.

I purchased Kendall a one –way ticket. If she feeds me the way that she's been teasing me, then I'm not letting her go back to Chicago. What was I going to tell Mya? She was so sick of hearing about another church conference out of town. Oh well, I definitely was not missing out on this fun-filled weekend. I was starving, if you know what I mean. I temporarily felt a twinge of guilt about my vows, my kids and my church but it didn't really matter. I had big plans for Ms. Kendall Scott. Who knows, maybe instead of just fulfilling my appetite, she would be the new and improved First Lady. The church would just have to get over it. A lot of the ladies did not take a liking to my wife anyway. I wondered why but then I thought back on the countless late-night "ministering" with the beautiful single females in the church. Oh yes, I knew exactly why they despised Mya.

The phone ringing snapped me back into reality. I smiled as the caller on the other end let me know everything was handled. A few hours later I quickly made another phone call trying to sound as convincing as possible. "Hello Mrs. Colbert, I'm so sorry to hear about Ahlisa's passing. Of course I will eulogize her," I said as I held back pure glee. "Please accept my condolences again. Did you receive the flowers that we sent? We're still in total shock as Ahlisa was a part of the family. I will continue to lift you and the family up in prayer." Great I thought to myself while I sang a little melody   "Ashes to ashes dust to dust anyone who crosses the great Pastor Robert B. Willoughby will end up in the grave it's a must".

I was elated Kendall would be here in a couple of days and the trash was taken out. Oh yes, my life was perfect.

JOSHUA LIVINGSTON

I was calling Ahlisa's phone but it constantly went straight to voicemail all week. Ahlisa knew what the plan was, so I wondered what was wrong. I was getting really worried, wondering if she had gotten caught or maybe she simply just couldn't go through with it and didn't know how to tell me. Afterall, I knew that she loved the family very much. It was not like her not to contact me back like this; maybe I should not have involved her.

My fiancée called me and said she had some exciting news to tell me. What my fiancée shared with me made my entire year. My dreams had finally come true.

Even if Ahlisa didn't get the information or the pictures, we just hit the Jackpot with this bit of information. I had been dating Ms. Madison Waters for two years now and we would soon be married. Madison was pressuring me for over a year now to make it official. I truly loved her but how could I stand before Pastor Willoughby as he officiates our wedding ceremony, knowing how he dishonors his marriage? This would draw a lot of attention with our members if he didn't marry us. If we eloped then the congregation who I truly considered my only family would be devastated. However, with the information I just received, everything would work out. That was when I remembered my favorite scripture.

Psalm 37: 7 "*Rest in the Lord and wait patiently for Him; fret not thyself because of him who prospereth in his way, because of the man who bringeth wicked devices to pass*".

MYA WILLOUGHBY

As I thought back over my life, I was saddened by the woman that I've become: scheming, lying, and conniving. This wasn't me: it sounded more like my husband. I had become a monster at the mere thought of being exposed. I did a lot of things that I deeply regretted but I could not be found out. What happened to the God-fearing, loving woman that I used to be? I still loved God, even though my actions didn't reflect it, but now "he" was trying to flip the script on me. *We had a deal and now because he found Christ, you want me to confess? Well, look how that ended up for you,* I thought.

I found Robert's bank statement and his itinerary for next weekend in his drawer. First-class ticket, five-star hotel and $10,000 for the very exclusive restaurant, Che' Campbell's, which we had not gone to yet. Robert told me about a convention of course and I didn't believe his lying behind. But now, I was even more intrigued to find out who was all this special treatment for. Robert was pulling out all the stops for this young lady. Robert left hours ago. I then decided that if this was how he wanted to play, let's play.

Three hours later, I checked into the hotel. It was not just any room mind you. I gave the concierge an additional $2,000 to bump Robert and his special guest out, which would tick him off. The great Pastor Robert Bradley Willoughby would be told no. "I wish I could have been there to see the look on his smug face," I laughed. Now, let's see who he's laying hands on this time.

ROBERT WILLOUGHBY

I checked into our room. I could have killed that little incompetent clerk at the front desk when I was told my room was mistakenly double booked. This was my favorite hotel, so they made it up to me. The room that I was given as an alternative choice was absolutely beautiful. Oh yes, Kendall was going to love this room. I sent for a Bentley to pick her up from the airport. This weekend would be a magical one I would never ever forget. There were flowers and candles everywhere. I had a trail of an assortment of pink and canary yellow diamonds leading straight to the master bedroom. I was longing for Kendall to arrive.

As soon as she walked into the room, I noticed that her body was amazing and she smelled great. Kendall was teasing me all night; there was no kiss and no touching while we were at dinner. She was different; not easy like the other ones and it captivated me. We went shopping, strolled through the park, and later returned back to the room. Now it's time for me to enjoy her. The lingerie she wore hugged and caressed every part of her toned body. It would not be on for long though as I kissed her passionately and touched her. I teased her until she was begging me and I loved every bit of it.

In all of the 45 years that I've been on this earth, this situation has never happened to me. Kendall was very calm and patient, telling me,

"It's ok baby, give it some time."

This was not the time for me to need a pill; it was highly embarrassing. Kendall started to do a little dance for me to help the situation but still nothing. Her body had no imperfections and she had the cutest green birthmark right on her inner thigh.

As Kendall seductively danced for me, the door violently swung open. I couldn't believe it. It was Mya standing at my door with a gun pointing towards the both of us. How did she know where I was? How did she get my room key? I never wanted Mya to ever catch me in the act. Mya was so shocked as she just stood there shaking. The gun trembled in her hands, her words I can still hear ringing loudly in my ears:

"ROBERT, SHE'S OUR DAUGHTHER!"

MYA WILLOUGHBY

I was shaking like a leaf as the gun trembled in my hands. Robert was shocked to see me to say the least. The beautiful girl who was giving Robert a seductive lap dance was indeed our daughter and I know that I had a lot of explaining to do. I thought back to that day in the coffee shop as I sat with "him" while he told me he felt so guilty about what we did. Years prior to our boys being born, I was pregnant. We were so excited but Robert only wanted a boy: a son, a Jr, an heir to the throne. Robert was so excited he raved about his son, his son, his son. The saddest day of my life happened while sitting in my Ob-Gyn, Dr. Scott's office. Dr. Scott said, "You're having a girl."

I sobbed uncontrollably and this confused Dr. Scott. "Mya, what's wrong? I thought you would be ecstatic especially due to your prior miscarriages"

I explained my dilemma to him and his response was so simple: "Meet me in the park after six tonight."

I knew it was an odd request but his voice was so soothing and calming so I quickly obliged. I trusted him; he has been my gynecologist for years.

In the park, Dr. Scott suggested that I deliver early via C-section and tell Robert I had a miscarriage. Dr. Scott's wife was unable to conceive, so they would raise her as their own daughter. I didn't want any updates, pictures, or information on my baby girl Olivia as that would have only made it harder on me. I felt that this was not only my best option but my only option. Robert was on a mission's trip to South Africa, I was eight months pregnant, so it was the perfect time for our plan. Everything went according to plan. I did not want to see her face nor hold her as it would only make this decision even harder. The only thing that I saw after delivering her was her tiny green birthmark on her right inner thigh as Dr. Scott took my daughter away from me forever. This haunted me every day of my life. On her birthday, I cried and stayed in bed all day. Throughout the years, Dr. Scott would send letters and pictures as well. I'm assuming because I've never opened them. I couldn't bring myself to open them but I often wondered how she was doing and how life was treating her.

Dr. Scott and his newfound family moved to Chicago once the baby had gotten stable. The only thing that I received in my private P.O. Box was my daughter's footprints and a letter from Dr. Scott informing me that they officially changed my baby's name from Olivia Rose Willoughby to Kendall Taylor Scott. As I sat across from Dr. Scott that day in the coffee house, I was looking at pictures of my daughter and all of her great accomplishments.

Dr. Scott wanted to inform Kendall of her true birth parents as the guilt that he and his wife felt consumed them greatly. He loved his daughter just as if she was his very own and he just couldn't lie to her any longer. I knew I could no longer convince him to keep quiet, nor could I change his mind. I persuaded him to come back to my private townhouse to speak with my husband. I knew what I had to do and I had to do it quickly. I didn't need to think twice.

I could imagine everyone's comments if they ever found out what I did, However, I had no other choice; the pressure to carry Robert's son was too much to bear. How would I ever explain to my only baby girl that the only father she had ever known was- GONE.

ROBERT WILLOUGHBY

“**M**ya, what in the world are you talking about? Whose daughter?” I asked as I scurried to put my robe on. I knew my cheating affected Mya tremendously but now she was just downright delusional. “Mya, we don’t have a daughter.”

By now, Kendall was fully dressed and staring at Mya as if she had two heads. The longing in Kendall’s face searched Mya’s eyes for validity. I looked closely and Kendall and Mya shared the same birthmark. Mya just stood there staring at Kendall as if she was in a trance. Kendall picked up her suitcase and stormed out, yelling from outside the penthouse, "LOSE MY NUMBER." Kendall took one last long look at Mya's face and stormed off, frantically reaching inside her bag for her cellphone.

I demanded an explanation from Mya and what she told me took all the air out of the room. Tears streamed down my face; I could not breathe or utter a single word. I got up, got dressed, removed my wedding ring, and dropped it on the floor. I had to get out of there, I had to think.

I went straight to the airport. As I sat in first class heading back to Atlanta, Mya's words haunted me over and over, and over again. Just the mere thought that I almost slept with my daughter caused me to run into the restroom and hurl. Mya had to pay, she will pay for this.

As I exited the plane and retrieved my car, I drove to the one person I still considered a friend.

Joshua Livingston

I was sitting in my living room going over the events for Pastor Rob's tribute service on Sunday. It's not anything that I desired to do but the congregation insisted we honor him for all the years of dedication and service. Pastor Rob paid for college tuition, mortgages, utility bills, gave away backpacks, even bought some members cars. The damage that he created was even greater in my opinion. Just then, my doorbell rang and the last person I thought that I would ever see at my door was standing there. As soon as I opened my front door, he collapsed on my floor, crying uncontrollably.

"What's going on?" I asked. I helped him up and guided him into my living room. I was worried because he was so weak and could hardly walk or speak. In all of my years of knowing him, I'd never ever seen him like this before. Pastor Rob ran into the restroom and began to hurl.

An hour later, he told me everything. I couldn't help but say, "Wow. A daughter, who you almost slept with; a daughter that you didn't know anything about, whom you flirted with and was thinking, could possibly replace your wife." I actually felt genuinely sorry for him and wouldn't wish this on anyone.

He apologized for everything and told me that he would formally step down at the tribute service. He then asked me to take over as head pastor. Here it was: he was handing me the opportunity I've been dreaming of for over ten years, yet I felt horrible accepting it. I told him that he could stay with me to clear his head because God knows that after all he's been through, I wouldn't want to go home either.

Four days later, Pastor Rob felt strong enough to go home. In those four days, we reconnected as friends and brothers in Christ. We prayed, read the bible, and watched television: we bonded. I just wanted to somehow take his mind off of what had just transpired.

After Pastor Rob left, my fiancée arrived shortly, excited to share with me all about her promotion.

"Babe this is great news," I said. "But what's the expose that you will be uncovering?" Madison retrieved a phone I've never seen before and handed it to me. My mouth hung open. There on the phone was a video of Pastor Rob and his former assistant, Jasmine Hills, doing things to each other that would make you ask God himself for forgiveness. I only wanted Jasmine to seduce him and get it on tape, not actually sleep with him. "You can't use this," I said, "not with everything that he's been through."

My fiancée was puzzled as she knew just how much I wanted to become the senior pastor. Madison replied, "This is the biggest story that Channel 61 has ever uncovered and Jasmine walked directly into my office and handed it to me. Once I showed my boss what I possessed, I received a promotion that I cannot and will not deny Joshua. **Channel 61 News** will be revealing the exclusive tape live on the air this Sunday on the 6:00pm news."

I told Madison everything that happened to Pastor Rob last weekend but she was heartless and cold. I begged and pleaded with her not to do it but Madison refused. I informed her that I could not be with a woman who would kick her very own pastor while he was down. This was Pastor Rob's lowest point and despite every obstacle or wrongdoing that he did, he deserved REDEMPTION. Pastor Rob deserved a second chance from all of us.

I called off my engagement right there in my kitchen and Madison was so heartbroken. She ran out of my apartment, leaving the phone behind with the video on it. I loved Madison, The Lord knows that I do, but could I marry someone so driven by tearing others down?

I picked up my phone to call her and that's when I saw a text from Madison. "I love you Joshua but you hurt me deeply. You have chosen your conniving pastor over the woman who's been there for you through thick and thin. Since you're so in love with Pastor Rob, press play for your viewing pleasure."

What was Madison talking about now? I had no desire to see him with Jasmine again but curiosity got the best of me. I clicked on the video and I dropped to my knees. It was Madison and Pastor Rob going at it right here in my very own bed. He had no mercy on my fiancée. Each thrust was worse than the one before and Madison was enjoying every moment of it. Rage exploded on the inside of me.

I called Madison. "SHUT UP and listen. Change of plans. Invite Channel 61 News to the Tribute Service on Friday and let's play the tape live and in living color in the church. I want the whole world to see, then zoom in on his face." I slammed the phone down while she offered a tearful apology. *OK Pastor Robert Willoughby, game on. I will show you once and for all who I really am.*

ROBERT WILLOUGHBY

I had not seen Mya since the day she told me we had a daughter and she wasn't answering any of my calls or texts. Mya had taken the children and left. The only reassurance I felt was knowing that she's an excellent mother and my boys would be fine. I had a lot of time to think and I knew that I could not forgive Mya. What she did affected not only me but she had ruined multiple lives with her lies. Kendall was not taking any of my calls. She was the main person that I wanted to apologize to but she would not give me the time of day.

With my tribute service being days away, I did not feel like celebrating much. I've deceived, misused, abused, hurt, and manipulated a lot of people. I did not think that kind of behavior called for a celebration. I truly was sorry for all the hurt and pain I caused. How could I make it right? Just then, I received a call from my favorite lady- my mom.

I came clean to my mom about everything and I do mean every intimate and sordid detail. She always gave the best advice. After I spoke, my mom simply answered, "Forgive."

I cried and poured my heart out for two hours and all she said to me was to forgive my wife. "Mom, did you hear what Mya did? I have a daughter, you have a granddaughter that you never got a chance to love, raise, and impart wisdom to, all because of Mya."

Then my mom told me, the pastor, about a scripture I was ignoring:

Ephesians 5:25 "Husbands, love your wives, even as Christ also loved the church, and gave Himself for it."

My mom continues, "What about my 'other' grandchildren whose lives were cut short by the hands of you, your mistresses, and the abortion clinic? I will only meet them in Heaven one day. You must forgive Robert. Forgiveness is not for the other person. Forgiveness is for you baby. Remember this verse my son

Matthew 6:14 KJV - For if you forgive men their trespasses, your heavenly Father will also forgive you."

"I know that scripture very well Mom but how do I forgive when I have been severely hurt by my very own wife, a person who claimed to love me forever, right before God? Mya would have probably never told me had she not followed me to the hotel."

Baby it won't be easy but true forgiveness is sometimes a process and you can do it. You not only need to forgive Mya but you need to forgive him."

"Who," I asked, confused.

"Your dad, Son-"

I stared at the phone, dumbfounded. Hearing my mom calling my name snapped me back into reality.

I can't believe my mother; she who was abused and manipulated the most by this man was now telling me that I had to forgive him. Then she hit me with the 'do it for me son.' She knew that I could never say no to her.

"One question Mom, how can you forgive the very same man who walked out on us for multiple women. He took care of other children while we struggled to eat, struggled to keep the lights on, and hiding from the landlord. I would never leave my family the way he did, so I can't forgive him."

"Robert, you left your family a long time ago. Only your physical body is there and even that's part-time. Honestly Son, I respect your dad for leaving us instead of staying there longer, inflicting more pain on us. Your dad informed me years ago that he could not stand the pain in my eyes any longer and that's the real reason that he left. Apparently you've gotten used to the very same look in Mya's eyes."

That last comment stung my heart to the core. Mom had a way of breaking me down and putting me back together like none other.

"Listen baby, it wasn't easy but I completely forgave your father. How can I say that I love God who I can't see but not forgive a person who I can see? Remember the scripture my love:

1 John 4:20 - If a man say, I love God, and hateth his brother, he is a liar: for he that loveth not his brother whom he hath seen, how can he love God whom he hath not seen?"

"Remember this Son, everyone and I do mean everyone, deserves **Redemption**."

Mom was right. In order for me to finally close this chapter, I had to go back to the root of my situation. I could not have this appetite trickling down to my sons. Everyone does deserve Redemption and I knew exactly what I needed to do.

JOSHUA LIVINGSTON

Everything was set for the tribute service for Pastor Robert. He was calling and calling but I refused to answer. He betrayed me for the last time; now this was personal. I rented the biggest screen projector I needed so everyone could see what their great pastor was truly capable of. I invited only the very elite to attend. It included the Mayor, Chancellor, Assemblymen: all the prominent men and women in Georgia. Everyone needed to know that he was capable of much more than just preaching. I had no proof whatsoever but I felt deep down he was behind the death of my friend and his nanny, Ahlisa.

My ex-fiancée wasn't getting off easily either; we will be debuting their video as well, unbeknownst to her. Madison needed to feel pain like I felt. All I've ever known was pain, rejection, and hurt in my life. I thought that she was added to my life to remove my pain, so never would I imagine that she would hurt me like none other. Why should I bear this pain alone? It was time for Madison and Robert Willoughby to be on the receiving end of my pain.

I had it all planned out to the tee. The emcee would announce "It's time for our video tribute of all the great accomplishments of Pastor Willoughby". I would then cue Channel 61 to go live and the world will see him and Ms. Jasmine Hills, then for the grand finale, Madison and Pastor Willoughby's tape would air. This will surely wipe that smug look right off of his pitiful face. The bonus would be Madison losing her job and all her credibility. I will show them once and for all what I'm truly capable of. Oh yes, the night will certainly be a night to remember.

ROBERT WILLOUGHBY

I don't know how I found myself driving to his house but the next thing I knew, I was anxiously pulling into his driveway. I hesitated. *What am I doing?* I thought. *I'm doing just fine without him.* I lied to myself. As I thought back on how I could've slept with my very own daughter, I quickly exited my car. The next thing I knew, I was ringing the doorbell to his townhouse. What stared me in the face was my very own reflection in twenty-two years. At sixty-seven-years-old, he was extremely handsome, dark, and tall at 6'9 and had a muscular build with the most beautiful set of white teeth I have ever seen. No wonder the ladies loved him. With years of sadness in his eyes, he invited me in.

An awkward silence filled the living room. I broke the ice and filled him in on my life since he wasn't man enough to raise me. Mr. Kenneth Mason Willoughby was a womanizer who was now old and all alone and if I didn't get my act together, this would be my end result. I spoke to him and filled him in on every dirty detail about my life, even my hatred for him. I informed him that it was only out of love and respect for my mother that I was meeting with him.

My dad began to cry hysterically, letting me know that no matter how hard he tried, he couldn't control himself and be with just one woman. He loved my mother more than any woman in the world and that's why he needed to leave since he couldn't give her what she needed. I was shocked after hearing him talk about his life. It resembled my life. Then he hit me with the 'he started going to church and gave his life to God.' He shared with his pastor all about his life, every embarrassing detail and instead of being shunned; his pastor took him under his wing and really mentored him. The pastor revealed to my dad that this wasn't just ill-behavior; his struggle was a result of a generational curse. Pastor Witherspoon let my dad know that sin travels. It travels from one generation to another whether you're raised with your parents or not. However, generational curses does not have to have the final say over our lives; they can be broken by deliverance and a decision. A decision to move in a different direction is what the Bible calls repentance. You make a decision to move towards God instead of away from Him.

"The same way you and I share the same DNA

Robert, unfortunately, we share the same spiritual DNA. I never told you to cheat on your wife, yet you have several times. My dad your grandfather also was a womanizer and he never instructed me to cheat on your mother but due to generational sin, I did. We all have hurt the women we love the most Son, you have done everything that I did to fail as a husband and father. You don't have to continue down this destructive path any longer. Make a decision today because we have to break this cycle. It has ruined too many lives and if you don't break this cycle now, it will pass down to your sons or even their children. Make a decision and truly repent to God with all of your heart and receive deliverance. Many people are suffering son with porn, drugs, lying, stealing, lust, depression, rejection and so many other battles, living their life in a repeated destructive cycle wondering why they can't get it right. Wondering over and over what's wrong with them. It's not them. It is a generational cycle that needs to be broken over their lives. It's going to be rough Robert but with Christ, all things are possible. I am begging you Son as I lay on my hands and knees. Will you? Can you ever forgive me? I don't know how much longer that I have on this earth but I would hate to know that I have two sons who want nothing to do with me."

By this time, I was falling apart, but as much as I tried to hate my father, I couldn't. I couldn't believe I had so much hate for him all these years when simply he was suffering himself. All I saw in his eyes was love and compassion for me. How could I ever not forgive him? "I forgive you Dad. I love you but you hurt us deeply. My mom would sob uncontrollably, holding your picture but I must release you from the space of hate that was in my heart as it's poisonous. I forgive you Dad and I pray that God forgives me also."

I hugged him tightly, not wanting to ever let him go. I collapsed in his arms. This was the embrace that I yearned for all of my life. But I remembered something he said and pushed him back suddenly. "What do you mean two sons? I am your only son."

My dad simply got up and retrieved his Bible. I saw my picture and then he held on to another picture tightly. "Son, I'm not proud of the things that I've done in my past and after I left your mother, I was in a very dark place. I was sleeping with multiple women and sadly some were even prostitutes. I had a relationship for about a year with this one prostitute in particular by the name of Janene. She ended up getting pregnant and we had a son."

I took the picture out of his hand and nearly stumbled to the ground. It was Joshua.

JOSHUA LIVINGSTON

The day had arrived for Pastor Rob's tribute ceremony. Everything was set in place; the church looked wonderful, the live band sounds were amazing, and the aroma of fine cuisine filled the air. The spirit of rage filled me to capacity. Oh yes, this would be a day to remember.

I reluctantly answered Pastor Rob's phone call but I did not want him to catch on to a thing. He said that he needed to talk to me immediately.

What happened now? I pondered. *Was someone else pregnant; who would I have the pleasure of escorting to the free clinic this time? Or did he need me to book a suite under his alias for his newest victim?* Whatever it was, I was through with being his accomplice.

"Yes Pastor Rob, I am at the church," I replied. "I wanted to get here hours early to ensure everything is running smoothly and according to plan," I added and mischievously smiled.

I have been calling Mya but she never answered. It was then that I was told that Mya had been gone for over three weeks now. She finally informed her husband that she and the children needed some time away as she couldn't bare the fact that she hurt him terribly.

Pastor Willoughby informed me that he would be here in fifteen minutes sharp to speak with me. This time was different and I could hear it in his tone of voice but I no longer cared about his well-being. I was too excited to give him this gift in front of the world.

I was greeted with a kiss. Jesus was also greeted with a kiss, so we both had a Judas in our lives. I asked, but really did not care how he was doing. We made small talk and it appeared as if he had been crying. However, his tears would not deter me at all. I was going through with the plan to destroy him, once and for all.

What Pastor Rob told me knocked all the wind out of me. The room went dark; my designer bow tie around my neck seemed to tighten on its own. I could no longer breathe and began to hyperventilate. I went outside momentarily to get some air and when I returned, I sat down and replayed what he said in my head.

"My father? You're my brother? W-w-what are you talking about?" I stuttered. "I don't have a father and my mother Janene died. She was a heroin addicted prostitute and I was told she never knew who my dad was. What kind of sick twisted game are you playing?"

Pastor Rob got up and left the room. He returned with the most handsome older black man my eyes had ever seen. My gray eyes met his tear-filled gray eyes. I had so many questions. Why now? Why today of all the days? I had a plan that I had to keep. I needed to destroy Robert Willoughby but now too many emotions flooded my mind.

"I need answers old man and I need them now," I demanded. The old man took out letters and pictures of my mother; he even had my official birth certificate. He informed me that my mom went to rehab that he paid for and she was doing great for the first year. But, I had so many complications due to her addiction that I had to have many surgeries. She could not take the stress and ended up back on drugs. This explained the scar right under my throat. No one had answers for me besides this man right in front of me.

My mother left me in the hospital and the clinical staff would not release me into her care. Since the old man was the one to sign my birth certificate he had it all this time. Due to his lifestyle he was unable to fully care for me and I was turned over to Child Protective Services. I went to a family that only cared about the monthly check that they received. I was a runaway at the age of thirteen and then I was sent to a group home. I received brutal beatings, starvation and experienced other things that were done to me that I would take to my grave.

The old man crying snapped me out of old memories. "I tried Son," he said, "but I had no rights. I tried my very best to find you but I failed. Your mother never gave you my last name since I was already married. I later found out through her old crowd that she overdosed on her twenty-ninth birthday. I prayed every day to God to help me so that I could see you again. I named you after my dad."

I was absolutely speechless. After all the years of hurt, pain, and anger of having no parents, shelter, hunger, abuse and molestation, now I find out that I actually have a father. I broke down because the pain was too much to bear. I didn't know how to process all this information. I was supposed to have Pastor Rob in pain and tears but here I was the one crying and feeling immense pain.

Although my tears were tears of relief; finally, questions that I've had for years concerning my parents were being answered.

I regained my composure and sat down as the room was still slightly spinning. Pastor Rob came back with some water which I quickly gulped down.

Our guests would arrive within the hour and we all had to get ourselves together. "Mr. Willoughby, if you would like to stay for tonight's ceremony, you're more then welcome to. Plus I have some more questions." I could not afford for him to leave and never have these questions answered, so I was ecstatic when he obliged.

They both left out to get properly dressed. By 8:00 pm sharp, all guests were in attendance and our Emcee was extremely entertaining: everyone was thoroughly enjoying themselves. By 9:15 pm, it was time for the video tribute. As the lights dimmed, I sat in between Pastor Rob and our father. A picture of Pastor Rob was displayed. With everything that I found out today, I could not go through with my plan. As devastated as I was, Pastor Rob brought healing to my heart by introducing me to my father. I raced to our media room to stop the video but I was too late. Pastor

Rob was there on the screen, his picture big and bold. I peeked into the crowd at my dad who was crying. What have I done? Then I looked at the screen and saw a beautiful picture of my mother. I was highly confused. What was going on? Madison appeared on the stage announcing, "On behalf of Pastor Robert Willoughby, we want to present Redemption Way Housing and Training Facility to the state of Georgia.

Redemption Way Housing and Training Facility will be forty newly constructed homes, a certified school with training and teaching facility, and a warehouse. This is where individuals who need a second chance in life will come. Whether they are suffering from homelessness, bankruptcy, drug abuse, being a single-parent, or straight out of prison, this will be a safe place for them to come. Redemption Way will provide food, shelter, wages, clothing, and training for the next three years. After your training, you will become certified instructors, real estate agents, and life coaches, who will bring in forty new people to receive training and job placement. This will be at the cost of Pastor Robert Willoughby and investors. This establishment is in loving memory of Ms. Janene Elaine Livingston."

Everyone cheered while Madison gave her speech. I was filled with mixed emotions of hurt, pain, joy and sorrow.

Pastor Rob approached me and told me that when I was not returning his phone calls, he spoke with Madison who filled him in on my revenge plan. *I guess Madison really did have a heart after all,* I thought.

"Joshua, although I did deserve revenge, I want to truly apologize as I was in a very dark place in my life. Can you ever forgive me?" he asked.

This act truly brought me to tears. "Today is the day for your celebration and to think that you thought so highly of me to bring me my father today. You knew what I was planning and instead of firing me or even yelling, you're here asking for my forgiveness. I wanted so badly to become the senior pastor and I was willing to do anything ruthless to take you down. The question is, can you ever forgive me brother?"

Pastor Rob replied, "I'm a pastor, a chosen vessel that God decided to use and I have done a lot of horrible things I'm not proud of. I've fully repented and asked God for total forgiveness and I know without a doubt that I am forgiven. There is nothing that we've done or will ever do that will make God not forgive us. Jesus while on the cross bore our sins, ALL of our sins, and every past, present, and future sin is forgiven. We can't out sin **HIS** perfect love that he has for us. HE doesn't care if you lie, cheat, or steal; whatever you have done, once you ask your heavenly Father for forgiveness, you will be forgiven. God sent his only begotten son Jesus on that cross to redeem us, so we are forgiven. Remember the Scripture

Ephesians 2:4-5 - But God, who is rich in mercy, for His great love wherewith He loved us. Even when we were dead in sins, hath quickened us together with Christ (by grace ye are saved).

"Our sins, my dear brother, have been forgiven. My mind, people, or Satan himself can't convince me otherwise. I've asked God countless times before for forgiveness. I've repented a million times to God saying, I'm sorry my Lord but I repented with my mouth only, never with my heart and never changing my ways. That is why I kept falling every single time. True repentance is not just guilt but a total change of mind and a total new way of living. This time, with my whole heart, I've truly repented." It doesn't matter what your title is, your financial situation, or what you have done, if you call on the name of the Lord, you will be saved. This is the Good News. Don't let anyone my dear brother Joshua tell you otherwise".

Romans 6:14 "For sin shall no longer be your master, because you are not under the law, but under grace".

"I was once told by a very wise woman that 'Everyone deserves REDEMPTION.' Joshua, I vowed to God that I would make things right, no matter the cost and that's a promise I intend to keep."

RESOLUTION

I thought long and hard on what I needed to do. As I walked inside the police station, I went straight to the officer's desk. I knew that this was the only way to make things right. My arrest would be broadcasted on every news station in Georgia. My face would be plastered on the front page of every newspaper in less than twenty-four hours, but nothing would deter me; not even the shame.

"I would like to turn myself in for murder. I have the gun, the location of the body, as well as pictures to prove my involvement."

The arresting officer looked confused and I'm sure it was because of my elite status. I was handcuffed and read my rights. In a final attempt to persuade me not to turn myself in, the officer said "Go home and think about this clearly". I'm sure it was because of the hundreds of thousands of dollars that we had given to the very same Police Department that warranted his concern. I assured Officer Warren James that I knew exactly what I was doing.

I was handcuffed and processed. As the officer led me down the long narrow hallway to my new home, the only thought that ran through my mind was

God, you will forgive me again, right?

PRAYER OF SALVATION

I (Insert your name here and make it personal) admit that I need you. This is not the life that you have destined for me. I ask that you forgive me of all my sins. I believe in my heart and confess with my mouth that Jesus Christ died for me and rose on the third day. By faith I receive You into my heart. I repent of all my sins. Deliver me from temptation and from the hands of the enemy. Cleanse me with your blood. Help me to live for you and only you.

If you said this simple prayer, I welcome you to the family. The Bible says,

"For whosoever shall call upon the name of the Lord shall be saved." (Romans 10:13)

If you prayed this simple prayer above and you are in need of direction, guidance or help finding a good church home, you can email me: blessedbeauty365@gmail.com.

This is the best decision that you will ever make.

God bless you.

About Author

Affectionately known as "Nicki" Nickita Campbell, she is an author and speaker. Nickita and her husband of nineteen years, Ricardo, are the proud parents of three children: Christopher, Elizabeth, and Elijah.

"Nicki" believes that having a strong support system has given her the courage to achieve her lifelong dream of becoming an author. With an amazing and extremely supportive husband that pushes her above and beyond her limits, she feels that there is nothing that she will not be able to accomplish. She also credits her parents Neville and Hope Thompson with being an anchor—especially her mom for playing a major role in the completion of this book.

Nickita wants to give a special thank you to her two brothers and two sisters. She loves you all and thanks you for always supporting her. Nickita also extends a very-special "thank you" to the two people that God has given charge of her spiritual well-being, Apostle Omar and Prophetess Makita-Lee Morton, along with her Kingdom Manna International Church family. Her love and appreciation also goes out to a great host of family and friends.

As a believer in and follower of Christ, "Nicki" believes that it is only through Him that all things are possible. This book is a testimony of what God can do through a yielded vessel.

9 781735 797700